Intergalactic Cop
Pursuit to Planet Earth

By:
Fred J. Richardson

Illustrated by Lynn Vellios

PublishAmerica
Baltimore

© 2006 by Fred J. Richardson.
All rights reserved. No part of this book may be reproduced, stored in a retrieval system or transmitted in any form or by any means without the prior written permission of the publishers, except by a reviewer who may quote brief passages in a review to be printed in a newspaper, magazine or journal.

First printing

At the specific preference of the author, PublishAmerica allowed this work to remain exactly as the author intended, verbatim, without editorial input.

All characters appearing in this work are fictitious. Any resemblance to real persons, living or dead, is purely coincidental.

ISBN: 1-4241-2618-5
PUBLISHED BY PUBLISHAMERICA, LLLP
www.publishamerica.com
Baltimore

Printed in the United States of America

Acknowledgements:

One of the responsibilities and joys of a grandpa is that of entertaining his grandkids with stories, and from this calling came the adventures of a boy, not so unlike my grandson, Will. This tale had its birth several years ago, was written and then forgotten. It was through the wonderful encouragement of my family that I resurrected the story, polished it some and asked them to give it an honest critique. They liked it and said it needed to be shared with lots of other young boys and girls whose fertile imaginations could easily place themselves in my hero's sandals. So, to my immediate family, my kids and grandkids, cousins and friends, I say, "Thank You" for believing that the stories I have to tell would be enjoyed by those other than my own captive audience.

No book by a new author could ever get off the launch pad without first catching the eye of the passing peruser, so the success of the writing effort can easily fall on the talents of the art work that goes into its cover. For this reason, I want to give a special recognition to Lynn Vellious, an art teacher, extraordinaire, of Glenco, Missouri, who developed all you see in the cover and the sketches with each chapter. Her perception for graphically depicting the themes has helped give the story a balance and completion. So thank you Lynn, you did a great job.

And finally, a special thanks to Tania Grab, Acquisitions Editor for PublishAmerica who thought enough of this work to help me get it through the myriad steps of publication. And a thanks to the PublishAmerica Company for heeding Tania's suggestion for acceptance.

Preface:

The human imagination cannot conceive of the many possible life forms that exist beyond the range of our earth's observations. When a young boy, on vacation off the coast of Maine, encounters a visitor from deep space, his own imagination and his life goes on a whirlwind ride that holds the balance between a world in chaos or one in peaceful ignorance of what might have been. He learns that just as all humans are neither good nor bad, so it is the same, with the myriad life forms that populate the universe.

Chapter 1
A Meeting of Minds

It was the first week of June and school vacation was just beginning. The sea gulls were having a raucous time as they skimmed the waters along Maine's Grand Manan Channel. The summer resort town had the distinction of being located on an island that was split in two by the Eastern and Atlantic Time zones. Half the population lived an hour behind their neighbors across the island, a fact which caused no end of confusion for the summer residents.

Tim walked along the shore with his terrier running tight circles around him, tempting him to try to catch or at least touch the jumping, little canine. It was a game the boy and his dog often played here at the beach as well as back home in Bangor. Tim saw their neighbor, old man Whitney, coming toward him walking face first into the brisk breeze blowing off the Atlantic, just as he did every morning at this time. The old man's golden retriever, Blondie, ran ahead of his master, running in and out of the surf, biting at the waves.

"Good morning, Mr. Whitney," yelled Tim, trying to make himself heard over the pounding of the early summer's surf that washed up at their feet.

"Back at'cha, sport," returned the old man.

"Say, Mr. Whitney, did you see the meteor shower last night?" Tim asked excitedly.

"Can't say that I did. Was she a big'un?" the old man replied.

"Well, there were only two meteors that I saw but they were sure bright. They were so big and lasted so long that they looked like they were going to come down right on this beach. If the wind and the surf hadn't been so loud I think I could have almost heard them hit."

The old man laughed and shook his head in amusement at the imagination of his young neighbor and headed on down the beach, calling his big dog out of the water. Tim looked around for his terrier, Barney, and found him investigating a gelatinous glob that looked like a jellyfish that had washed ashore. He called the dog away for fear the sea creature would sting the dog's nose. He looked around for a piece of driftwood with which to examine this mystery from the deep, and finding a piece of lathe that had washed ashore, he went over to his dog, who seemed to have now lost the object of his curiosity. Tim joined Barney in his search but soon abandoned the quest and assumed it had washed back out to sea. With their morning adventure completed, the two companions found their way back home and to the kitchen where Tim's mother was just taking some cookies out of the oven.

"I thought the smell of fresh-baked cookies would bring you two in," Mrs. Northfield said, as she set a plate of a half-dozen steaming, TollHouse cookies on the table.

"Mom, you're an angel," he said, as he picked up a handful and headed for his room. "I'm going to work on that computer class that we'll be starting in September. Maybe I can get a jump on the other freshmen," he added as he walked away munching a warm cookie.

Tim sat in front of his computer watching the screen as it booted up. Barney had jumped up to put both front feet on Tim's leg and assumed his typical look of pleading for one of the treats that Tim seemed to be jealously guarding. Tim yielded to his friend's begging while watching the screen come to life. Suddenly Tim's leg felt warm and moist as though Barney had "initiated" him, just as the dog had done on numerous occasions when he was just a small puppy on Tim's lap. Tim quickly brushed Barney's feet down and looked at his trousers, but there didn't appear to be anything amiss. Putting the incident out of his mind, he began concentrating on the computer screen. He was exploring several programs and began working on a history research project he had started earlier and placed in a file for future use. As he studied the screen, he realized he was having trouble focusing on the script. He batted his eyes, then rubbed them to try to clear the "cobwebs". After a few seconds his vision returned clear as though nothing had happened. He wondered if he was getting to a point where he would need glasses. He prayed that this was not the case because wearing glasses and playing basketball just didn't work all that well. He remembered how some of his friends had to wear glasses and they were always getting knocked off and broken during the games. No. He did not want glasses. Still....what had caused his vision to blur so suddenly? Maybe it was just the salt air from his morning's excursion.

He spent the next hour reading material from cyberspace. History held a fascination for him and he often lost track of time as he explored with the early pioneers, or sought pirate fleets off the coast of Europe, or visited early American Indian tribes with the Lewis and Clark expedition as they searched for a better passage to the northwest. Eventually, the exertion from the morning's jaunt along the shore and the mental efforts of his work on the computer began to take its toll, and he felt the best remedy was one more cookie with a nap to follow.

His head had no sooner found a comfortable notch in his pillow than he was sound asleep. He began to come out of his sleepy fog when Barney, who was sitting on the foot of his bed, decided to scratch an itch. Tim lay for a moment trying to recall the elements of the dream he had been having just before Barney interrupted his slumber. He faintly recalled seeing lines of written words running in a continuous stream across his mind's eye. He concluded it must have been something induced by his reading at the computer just before taking that nap. Sure, that's what it was. He was reliving his study work. But there was something strange in recalling what he had read. It didn't seem to make any sense, nor did it seem to be related to the history project he was working on. He guessed it was like so many dreams that simply float away into a maze after you have been awake for a while. In an hour he probably wouldn't recall anything he had seen.

He got up from his bed and headed back to the kitchen for some more cookies but his mother limited him to just three more because lunch would be in an hour and she didn't want him to spoil his appetite. Boy, what a joke that was, he thought, as he picked up his basketball and headed out to the garage where his dad had put up a net and backboard. He and Barney had a daily game where he tried to dribble around the dog and break for the basket. The dog had picked up on the rules fast and it became more and more difficult to fake him out and make it to the basket without the dog hitting the ball with his foot or just running over the top of it. Tim and Barney had squared off as Tim made a fast break to the dog's left and at the last second turned to his right, but Barney was ahead of him and ran squarely in front of a surprised Tim. The unfortunate aspects of having an opponent that was so short, as well as fast, was that sometimes Tim would go end-over-teakettle and find himself sprawled on the ground. This time Tim landed knee-first on the concrete driveway. There was an immediate pain as he rolled onto his back, but surprisingly, the pain went away just as quickly. He was just getting to his feet when his mother called him to come in for lunch. As he headed for the bathroom to clean up, his mother stopped him, and frowning, looked at his trouser leg, which had a hole at the knee.

"Tim," she cried, "what happened to your leg? You're bleeding." Tim looked down at his jeans and sure enough, there was a bit of blood on the knee. He pulled up his pant's leg to see why he was bleeding in the absence of any pain. There was no sign of a cut or abrasion or any indication that he had been injured. "Where did the blood come from, Tim?" his mother asked.

"I don't know, Mom. I must have done it when I fell. Barney fouled me when the ref wasn't looking and I took a little tumble, but I'm fine. It doesn't hurt," Tim explained.

"Well, go get cleaned up. I just don't see how you could grind the knee out of your pants without skinning your leg," she replied, shaking her head.

After lunch, Tim decided to return to his computer for a while and was in the middle of reading about the early fur trappers of his native state, when across the screen appeared the words,

"We must communicate."

Tim was taken back as he read the sentence, for it was superimposed over the text already on the screen. His first thought was that someone had hacked into his computer and sent the message, but as he looked aside, the message remained in the same place in his vision, front and center. He shut his eyes and shook his head but he could see the same words with his eyes closed. His heart began to race as he felt a moment of fright not knowing what was causing this illusion. He thought, perhaps he had hit his head without realizing it, when he fell over Barney. His heart was racing so he took a deep breath and tried to relax. He looked back at his monitor and the illusion was gone so he settled back in his chair and tried to phantom what had just happened. Just as he was beginning to think his eyes had simply been playing tricks on him, another message appeared just as before. This one read,

"I'm sorry for causing you discomfort. I mean you no harm. We must communicate."

Tim jumped up from his desk and bolted into the kitchen where his mother was cleaning up the last of the lunch mess and visiting with Tim's dad, who had just come back from the mainland. Trying to control the quiver in his voice, he asked his mother if she could see anything wrong with his eyes. She looked closely at both eyes, and then his dad took a look. Both agreed that he looked perfectly normal and asked what caused his concern. He explained that he was seeing words floating across his vision that were unattached to anything. They looked at each other and frowned as worried parents might do when faced with a question for which they have no answer.

"Maybe you ought to lay off the computer for a while, son," his dad advised. "It sounds like a case of eye strain to me."

Tim turned and slowly walked back to his room where he immediately shut down his computer. He picked up one of his favorite books, *Undaunted Courage,* by Steven Ambrose and began reading about exploration of uncharted territories. Suddenly, another message appeared in his line of vision. This time it sent chills down his back because of the personal nature of the message, which read,

"Tim, do not be afraid. You are in no danger. Relax and we will communicate."

Tim tried to jump off the bed but found his legs wouldn't move. Then another message appeared.

"I'm sorry I had to immobilize you, Tim. Do not be afraid. I can not hurt you. We must communicate."

Strangely enough, Tim wasn't as frightened as he had been earlier. Maybe he was getting used to this mysterious writing. He sat very still for a moment collecting his thoughts about him. Was this some weird misfiring going on in his brain, or was it an attempt by some dead spirit trying to get in touch with him. He recalled reading about such phenomena but had never known anybody who had actually experienced it. He decided to test this, whatever it was, and see what happened. Softly, he asked,

"Who are you?" Immediately a message appeared across his vision.

"In your language I would be called 'Hunter'. Where I am from, my identity is more of a thought than a sound. There is much I need to tell you and I need your help in a matter of the greatest importance to your world as well as my own." With that, the message disappeared. Tim sat motionless for what seemed a very long time but in reality was less then a minute. Finally, he had formulated what he considered the question that might unravel some puzzles for which he had no answers.

"What exactly are you?" he inquired. Tim began to read the reply.

"The exact nature of my existence is difficult to explain, in that your planet does not have any organisms similar to me, but I'll try to make you understand as best I can. Those of my world have no specific shape. We are more similar to a gelatinous matter than to a rigid structure. We extract oxygen from our surroundings, which is why I can survive on your planet. We require a host for mobility and in exchange for this symbiotic relationship, we protect our host from harm. Our civilization is several billion years older than this planet's and my home planet is more than 10,000 light years from here. So, you see, there are vast differences between us."

Tim realized his one question, which he had hoped would clear this up, only created a hundred more questions, and he didn't know where to begin.

"Don't get excited, Tim. Your heart rate is accelerating and it's making it very noisy in here. Be calm. Take a deep breath and let it out slowly." Suddenly, the words made it quite clear that whatever this thing was, it was inside of him and now his heart rate did jump. Then an unexpected calm came over him. The message explaining his sudden change in physiology began to scroll across his vision.

"Tim, it is my duty to protect you since you are my host, therefore, I've just reduced your heart rate and released some endorphins to calm you. I realize this is both a shock and a surprise for you, but please trust that I can do you no harm. I must have you calm so that we can come to know and understand each other."

"OK," Tim ventured aloud, "if you are all you say you are, how is it you are able to write your messages in my line of vision? Where did you learn our language and did you somehow do something to my knee when I fell? Why is your name Hunter?"

"To answer your question about my means of communication, let me say that this was just to introduce myself, in the least disturbing manner I could create. I prefer telepathy but I wasn't sure how you would react if you suddenly started hearing voices in your head. Your culture is still a long way from nonverbal communication. I saw that you were a reader so I chose a written message. As to how I knew about your planet and its people, that's simple. We have been observing this planet since its creation but it was only since you developed the means of wireless communication that we have been able to tap into all the various aspects of each of your distinct cultures. Your use of what you call cyberspace and satellite communication has been the real boon to the other cultures living among the millions of other galaxies scattered throughout the universe. The information available to you has also been available to me. I am familiar with every language on this planet and can communicate with anyone because we use telepathy, which deal with thought patterns rather than spoken phrases. As for your knee, yes, I healed it but not before a small amount of your fluid leaked out. I am sorry I was not faster to protect you from falling but as I had never had a human for a host I was unprepared for your sudden shifting in movement. Incidentally, I was able to enter your body by using the quadruped you have for a companion. I encountered him when I came out of the water. I had seen the two of you running and thought at first, he was the superior life form since he was faster. I guess I needed more research on your planet's inhabitants. But when I realized he could neither speak nor read I took the first opportunity to leave him and adopt you as my host. I entered your right leg when he put his feet on you. In answer to my title, I am called Hunter since that is what I do. I am what you would call a policeman. I hunt down criminals from my world or any other world that hires me."

"Oh," Tim said, "You're like some intergalactic cop. Is that right?"

"Pretty close," the message scrolled.

"Well, what are you doing here?"

"I crashed my ship here last night while chasing a fugitive from my own planet. He also crashed right ahead of me. I have been pursuing him for about five of your centuries. He tried to use the gravitational pull of your planet to act like a sling shot to give added boost in launching out of this system but that requires a very delicate maneuver with precise timing. It's necessary to catch the rotation at the exact point to maximize your thrust out and be flung into space at near the speed of light. Once away from your gravitational pull, we can accelerate to several times the speed of light. But to put it very plainly, we just got too close. It's that simple. He kept getting closer and I wouldn't back off, so we both crashed."

Tim's eyes lit up with the realization that he had witnessed the crash last night in what he thought was a meteor shower.

"You're right, Tim. Those were our ships last night. We made entry on a long, shallow, sloping descent and landed in about 25 meters of water, on what your maps identify as a continental shelf."

Tim jerked upright.

"How did you know I had realized I'd seen you crash? I didn't say anything."

Hunter added, "But you thought it, Tim. Remember, I said we use telepathy. I read your thoughts, and I'll teach you to read mine. It will make communications much easier."

"Wow! Wait until Mom and Dad get a load of this. This is so far out that it's in a land of its own."

"I'm sorry Tim, but this is something we have to keep between us until I locate my prey. He is somewhere around here and I must find him and destroy him. Even though he and I are of the same life form, he will not hesitate to kill his host if it will serve his purpose. This is but one of the many crimes for which I pursue him and he must be destroyed. Your own culture has produced and continues to produce many, which are totally evil. If Torg, for that is his name, were to find a host who was as evil as he is, the damage they could do is unimaginable. And he will simply go from host to host until he finds one like himself. But he will most likely kill each one he leaves, to cover his tracks."

"You mean I can't even tell my folks?" Tim asked.

"Especially not your folks. If Torg has found one of them for a host and he finds out you are my host he will surely kill them. We must stalk him without his knowing I am here."

"Well, if he is hiding in someone how will we know where he is?"

"There are ways," Hunter answered, "but first of all, we have to work on teaching you to communicate with me without speaking. The time may come when we will need to talk to each other but would not want someone close by to know it."

"You know something, Hunter?", Tim said with excitement in his voice, "this could be a real help at exam time." Although Tim didn't see any words floating before his eyes he had the distinct feeling he heard someone laughing.

Chapter 2
Seeking the Prey

After supper that evening, Tim took Barney and headed for the beach where they had first encountered Hunter. The evening surf had quieted down considerably, which was typical of this area along the northern seaboard. Tim was still vocalizing his words to Hunter even though Hunter had already understood Tim's thoughts before they were spoken. The idea of telepathic communication was so new to Tim that he found it difficult to adjust to the concept. Hunter on the other hand was using his skills more and more to impress his message into Tim's conscious thoughts. As a training technique, the alien would imprint the message across Tim's view for him to read, but would send the same thoughts slightly ahead of the written words. This created a sort of mental echo and Tim slowly began to depend on his thoughts and less on reading the scrolling letters. They walked along the beach conversing, more to practice their technique than to convey any vital information. At one point Tim stopped and wondered if this were all some elaborate dream from which he would soon awaken. Would he then discover that he was just plain Tim, instead of, Tim Northfield, host to a space traveling alien who could talk to him through telepathy and keep him from being injured and do, who knows what more? Instantly, Tim received his answer from Hunter.

"It is no dream, Tim, and there are so many more things I can do to help you. And for this, I ask your help, in return."

Tim was a little unnerved to realize that this thing inside him could read every thought he had. He wondered if he was never to have a truly private moment again. His answer was immediate.

"Think of me as an extension of your subconscious that just bleeds over into your conscious. Don't feel that I am in any way infringing on your privacy. I make no judgments about what you do but I am obligated to intercede if I see harm coming."

It was then that Tim realized he and Hunter had been communicating without Tim saying anything or having to read the scrolling letters.

"Hey, we can talk without talking," Tim shouted and jumped a spinning pirouette down the beach.

"It's a matter of concentration, Tim," Hunter explained. "As soon as you stop concentrating on the technique and begin to use the ability you already possess, it will happen. We are now past the first hurdle, so it's time to get to work."

"Tell me what you want me to do, Hunter, and I'll try my best", Tim assured. Hunter began to outline their plan.

"First, we have to assume that Torg survived the entry and crash. Then we must figure how he might have acquired a host. He was no more than a couple of your minutes ahead of me, so I will assume we made it to the shore about the same time. Can you recall seeing anyone else along the beach at that same time?"

"Yes! As a matter of fact old Mr. Whitney was walking his dog. We stopped and I told him about the meteor shower that I thought I had seen the night before. His Lab, Blondie, that's his dog, was running into the water and biting at the waves. Do you think Torg could have gotten into Mr. Whitney's dog like you had gotten into Barney?"

"It's very possible, Tim," Hunter thought. "Perhaps the dog wasn't biting at the waves. Maybe he saw something floating in the water and thought it was something to eat. At any rate, if Torg did take the dog for a host, it wouldn't have taken him long to discover as I did, that being faster doesn't always make for the best host. Let's see if we can find Mr. Whitney and the dog."

"Could the dog have killed Torg if he ate him," Tim wondered silently.

"No, because we have no solid structure. He could have allowed himself to be swallowed or simply absorbed through the dog's skin, as

I did with you. For now, let's find Mr. Whitney, but when we do, just act normal, as though you've come by for a visit. And don't make physical contact. If Torg is using him for a host and you touch him, Torg will know where I am. I would rather watch the older man and try to determine if he has been invaded. Torg would not expect me to be working with a host's knowledge of my presence so soon after our arrival. Surprise is the element in our favor."

They continued down the beach until they came to an older but neatly kept white cottage sitting behind the usual white picket fence typically found in this part of Maine. Tim approached the open porch and called Mr. Whitney's name. The old gentleman came to the screen door and after recognizing Tim, stepped outside and invited his young neighbor in for a cold glass of tea. Smiling, Tim stepped inside being careful not to touch his host. Sitting down at the little kitchen table, Tim asked where the big golden Lab was.

"Blondie's laying down right now, Tim. She took a bad spell this morning and for a while I thought I was going to lose her. I think she may have had a seizure of some kind. She was staggering around the room, and then collapsed. I picked her up and ran out and got in the truck and took her down to the end of the island where Doc Mathers has a place. He's a baby doctor but I thought he might be able to help. But, by the time we got there Blondie was pretty much her old self again. I was too embarrassed to even take her in to see Doc after she come to so quickly. Besides, I was kind of anxious to get back home 'cause I thought the poor old girl had lost control of her bladder when I was carrying her. But, it must not have been much 'cause I couldn't find where she soiled my clothes at all. But it sure got my attention."

Suddenly, Tim was most anxious to get away from the old man's house. Hunter was telling him what he had already surmised. That moist, warm sensation was when Torg had left the dog and entered the old gentleman's body. Any action on their part right now could mean sure death to Tim's kindly neighbor. Excusing himself with the story that he had to get back home, Tim stood and turned quickly leaving the house and an unsuspecting Mr. Whitney. Tim ran about a hundred yards down the beach as fast as his legs would take him. He wanted to put some distance between Torg and Hunter, as well as himself. He stopped and turned, looking back up the beach as the last fading light of the day disappeared over the mainland. He was about to discuss the situation with Hunter when he realized he wasn't panting from the exertion of the run. Tim had never been very athletic and a touch of asthma had always prevented him from performing well in strenuous sports. But now, his legs didn't feel as though he had just run a hundred yards at full speed, and come to think of it, that was some pretty impressive speed at that. Hunter, anticipating his question, explained that he was obligated by a culture thousands of generations old to protect his host from harm. In this case, it involved increasing the oxygen rich blood to Tim's lungs and to his muscles, thereby enabling him to run much faster than normal without the usual signs of fatigue.

"This just gets better and better, Hunter. What other surprises do you have for me? Will I be able to leap tall buildings in a single bound?" he asked half jokingly.

"Why would you want to do that?" came the silent reply.

"I'm sorry. That was a human's joke. It refers to this alien that comes from a distant galaxy and crash lands on Earth. He has powers beyond the normal human's and he works to right the wrongs of this planet while trying to keep his own identity a secret."

"Well, I can see a familiar theme here, Tim, but I guess one must be human to see the joke aspect of it." Now it was Tim's turn to enjoy a silent laugh.

Chapter 3
New Skills, New Thrills

When Tim walked back into his house, his dad greeted him at the door with, "Where you been, Scout?"

"I walked down to Mr. Whitney's. His dog has been sick but he seems to be doing better," Tim replied.

"Yeah, George said he thought he might have had a seizure. He's getting up in years and those things do happen."

"Are you talking about Mr. Whitney or his dog," Tim inquired.

"I suppose it's true of both of them but I was talking about the dog. I guess I should have said, 'She's getting up in years'."

Suddenly a thought came to him and Tim wasn't sure if it was his own or from Hunter.

"Uhh, Dad, when did you talk to Mr. Whitney?"

"I gave him a lift to the drug store on the north end just before lunch. Why do you ask?"

"Oh, no reason. It's just that Mr. Whitney never mentioned it when I was up at his place this evening. No reason. I was just curious," Tim replied with a feeling of foreboding in his stomach. As he turned to leave, Tim said over his shoulder that he was going to work a while on a computer program, then go to bed. Tim stepped into his room, shut the door and sat down heavily on his bed.

"What do we do now?" he thought. "If Dad was in contact with Mr. Whitney, Torg could have taken him for a host."

"Be calm, Tim. Let's look at the possibilities. First, Torg may still be in Mr. Whitney. We'll just have to take the risk and go back there and I'll go into him and find out. You'll have to let me leave your body where I can then go right into his. I'm not sure I can kill Torg while he is using a host. It poses a risk to the host and I'm not able to take that risk. Also, you must not come in contact with the old man before I'm prepared, or with your dad, for that matter. Torg could absorb into you in a matter of a couple seconds. We must go to Mr. Whitney's tomorrow and pick our opportunity. Right now, you need your rest. Your body is signaling for a sleep period. We'll pick this up again tomorrow morning. But in the mean time, do not touch anyone," cautioned Hunter.

"Fat chance I have of falling asleep with you racing through my mind, figuratively and literally," Tim declared. A silent message said,

"You assume a resting position, Tim, and I'll help you achieve an unconscious state."

Tim put on his pajamas, climbed into bed and flexed his shoulders one time, and was in a deep sleep.

The interval between lying down and waking up, seemed like a nanosecond to Tim, when in reality it was nearly 10 hours. Hunter's studies of earth's life forms had taught him that before humans reached their full maturity they required considerable periods of unconscious rest. When necessary, with Hunter's help it would be possible for Tim to skip sleep all together, since the alien could alter his metabolism without endangering his health. This was one of the benefits of their interdependent relationship that he would eventually explain to Tim. But for right now, he didn't want to alter or disturb any of Tim's normal behavior, at least so far as would be noticed by his parents.

When his sleep ended, Tim was completely awake and alert. As he recalled all the events of yesterday he could hardly believe that so much of his life had changed in the span of two dawns. His first telepathic communication of the day was to inquire as to whether his new passenger was awake. The answer came immediately.

"We do not have periods of unconsciousness, Tim. This is primarily an Earth thing."

"You don't ever sleep?" Tim asked with amazement. The alien silently explained,

"It isn't necessary, since an organism such as I am, can rejuvenate itself at will."

"Do you eat and drink?" inquired Tim. Hunter patiently answered,

"As my host, Tim, your body provides me with all the nourishment I require. And I absorb liquid from what you ingest." This posed a delightful question for Tim.

"Will I have to eat more now that I'm feeding you as well?"

Tim imagined a laugh coming from his new guest and surmised that aliens must have a sense of humor.

"Judging from the quantity of food you consumed last evening," Hunter added, "I would say there would likely be little notice given to the amount necessary to sustain my needs. Speaking of which, your digestive system is indicating it is time for you to feed yourself once again. Strictly as an observation, how often do you feed yourself?"

"We have three regular meals a day and a couple of snacks, like the cookies we had yesterday. Then sometimes I will eat something before I go to bed. Does that pretty well answer your question?"

"Most assuredly," Hunter replied. "Now I'm sure no one will notice your eating a bit more for my needs." They both laughed at the humor of their conversation but Tim couldn't refrain from a very audible chuckle. He thought he might have to work on that to prevent some uncomfortable stares from those around him.

With breakfast finished, Tim asked his mother if he might go to Mr. Whitney's to see how the old man's dog was doing. She said it was fine but he should be home by noon for lunch. Tim jumped on his bike and headed for his neighbor's house. When he arrived at Mr. Whitney's cottage, he found it empty. He called through the screen door not really knowing what he would do if the old man were home. He was almost relieved to discover neither the man nor his dog was to be found.

"What now, Captain?" thought Tim. He received the silent response stating,

"Thanks for the promotion. As a hunter, I don't expect to be what you call a Captain for another hundred years or so, but for now, since we can't get to the old man, can we go out to where my ship crashed?" inquired Hunter.

"We have a small fishing boat," Tim answered, "but what good will that do us?"

Hunter took a moment before answering.

"Do you have anything to protect your eyes from the salt water? It might be easier for you to provide that protection since I will be busy with other, more important work."

"Sure, I have a swimming mask I use when I snorkel," Tim explained. Snorkel was a term Hunter had not come across in his studies of earth and its inhabitants, so Tim got to give a lesson, of sorts, to his otherwise, intellectual superior. Hunter said he would show Tim another way their new relationship would benefit each other but they needed to get out to the crash site. The many islands that dotted the coastline would make it easier to locate the spot. Tim decided not to ask his mother for permission to take the boat out, as he was quite sure she would say "no" since he would not be with his father. Even though Tim knew how to handle the boat, his folks hesitated on turning him loose with it knowing how treacherous the Atlantic could become on a very short notice. In addition there was the Whirlpool to consider. It was said to be the largest whirlpool in the Western Hemisphere and at times the current being sucked into its center was so great that even large vessels with huge engines were no match for it. Now that Tim thought about it, it seemed those balls of fire he watched were in the general direction of the Whirlpool. Hunter was analyzing Tim thoughts. He told his host that he had detected an unusual current in the water shortly after the crash. As his craft was breaking up, he had jettisoned the cabin away from the main body of the craft and had hit the water at least eight thousand meters beyond his ship. He calculated that had he stayed with the main part of the ship he might have been closer to that point where the current was being pulled.

Tim retrieved his swimming mask and trunks from his room and rode over to the community boathouse where his dad kept their boat. It was a simple fishing boat like so many found along the Atlantic coast. It was a Boston Whaler, seventeen feet long, with a fifty horsepower motor. Tim lifted the six-gallon gas tank and discovered it was less than half full. They would need at least a full tank as well as a spare to make the round trip to their destination through Cobscook Bay. He started the motor and pulled over to the gas pier to get the fuel. The attendant came out and began filling the boat's fuel tank. Tim lifted the extra tank up onto the dock and asked the deck hand to fill this one as well. Just as the tank neared full, the deck hand pulled the nozzle out to check the volume. The gas hit the side of the tank splashing up onto Tim's hand and arm. There was an instant ringing in his ears, almost like a cry. Tim backed away from the attendant and reached down into the water to wash the gas off his arm. Tim anxiously asked Hunter if the sensation he had just experienced was coming from the alien's thought patterns?

"Didn't that hurt when that liquid hit your arm?", Hunter inquired.

"Not really", Tim replied. "It stings a little and stinks a lot, but I washed it off right away. Why? Did it cause you pain?"

"Yes! A lot of pain. But the pain left as soon as I retreated back inside several centimeters. What exactly was that?" came the silent inquiry.

"Gasoline. It's what we use to power the motor. Are you unfamiliar with petroleum?", asked Tim, with slight disbelief. Hunter explained,

"I've read the material about petroleum in the accounts of this planet but I've never encountered it before. Tell me, Tim, is it easy to acquire this material?"

Without indicating conversation, Tim explained the process of buying gasoline at filling stations or at refueling docks. Hunter seemed unusually interested but let the subject drop for the time.

The two adventurers, human and alien, headed out into the western edge of the Bay of Fundy, keeping the chain of islands between themselves and the open sea, just for safety's sake. Suddenly, Hunter told Tim to stop as they were nearly at the site where his cabin craft had gone down. Tim looked around and could see nothing distinctive about this particular spot.

"How do you know it's right here, Hunter? We're a long way from any particular island." Hunter paused for a moment to select a way to explain without insulting the life form his host represented.

"Our species have developed many abilities throughout time which you could not possibly recreate for yourself, but we can determine where we are in relationship to other areas, specifically, in outer space or on a planet."

"Oh, you mean like a GPS. That's a Global Positioning System. We have them here. They gives positions based on coordinates from a series of satellites," Tim replied, with a bit of prideful boast in his thoughts.

"Something like that, Tim," Hunter came back, "except my system is built in."

"Does this mean I can never get lost?" Tim asked, half jokingly.

"That it does," Hunter assured his young host.

"Cool," Tim thought. Hunter immediately asked,

"Are you cold, Tim? I didn't detect any indications of discomfort."

"No, no," Tim responded. "It's a figure of speech. It means, that something is good. If it's cool, it's good. See?" After digesting this concept, Hunter replied, "It appears I've much yet to learn. But that's cool." They both enjoyed a silent laugh.

Hunter instructed Tim to drop an anchor to maintain their position. The twenty- pound weight hit the water with a big slash and immediately began dragging the hundred feet of rope over the side. Finally, the rope went slack with about fifteen feet of line left. Tim let the boat drift with the wind until the line was taut and the boat held its position.

"What now, Captain?" Tim inquired. Hunter casually replied,

"Now, we will go down and check on my craft."

"Whoa! Hold the phone!" Tim cried out loud. "Do you realize just how cold that water is? It can't be more than 65 degrees. Man, I wouldn't last five minutes in there. And there is no way I could dive to the bottom. We better rethink this whole adventure."

"I'm sorry, Tim," Hunter calmly said with consoling reassurance. "I'll explain how this will work. First of all, I will keep you from feeling the cold of the water by covering your exterior with my own body. I'll use your own metabolism to increase your body temperature and it will feel as though you are in a warm bath. The biggest change I'll make is to extract oxygen from the water itself and convert it to a gas and fill your lungs after you exhale. You have your eye protection so I think we're ready to go check on my cabin craft." Tim slowly pondered what his companion had just explained.

"You can do all that?" Tim finally asked.

"Yes, it really is more simple than you imagine, Tim," came the silent reply. "But Tim, I'm not clear about the phone you mentioned," the alien added.

"Oh, that's just another expression. I got it from my dad. He says it when he wants someone to stop and think about something for a moment. It's like 'cool'. It has nothing to do with the literal meaning of the word. You have to consider the context in which it is used to know what it implies. Understand?"

"I'm beginning to realize communication may involve more than simply knowing the meaning of a word. Your species seems to have implied meanings, as well," Hunter answered.

"We'll work on that later," Tim replied anxiously.

"Let's get wet. I want to see how this thing is going to work."

"Don't be alarmed by the appearance of my body covering yours," Hunter advised. "So just get into the water and wait a moment while I adjust to create your oxygen." Tim was intrigued as he saw his skin take on a glossy finish. He thought he must look like he had been varnished. He touched his bare arm and felt a soft jelly-like substance.

"Is that you, Hunter?" Tim inquired, as he continued to poke himself. He heard a silent reply that he was in fact touching an area of the alien's body. Tim smiled almost in disbelief at the wonder of his circumstance and cautiously slipped over the side into the chilly water. He was still anticipating the sting he usually felt when he would venture into the surf with his friends. It was a pleasant surprise to find that Hunter knew what a warm bath was supposed to feel like. He carefully put his face into the water, peering through his dive mask down into the blue-green depths.

"Go ahead and exhale, Tim," Hunter said silently, "and then feel your lungs reinflate." Tim did as instructed and felt his lungs fill with air just as though he had taken a deep breath.

"Wow! Now we're cookin'," Tim thought. "Hunter, you have no idea what a change you are going to make in my life. I've never been much for out-door sports. I never could run very fast. And now I can swim like a fish. This is just awesome."

"Don't get too carried away, my young friend," Hunter cautioned. "Remember, no one must know about me and if you start doing things you've never been able to do before, questions will arise. We must be cautious in all you do, like right now. Take hold of the rope you threw into the water and follow it to the bottom. My craft should be close by."

Tim began a descent, looking all around him into the clear green world that lies just out of reach to those who are afraid to venture into this nether realm. As he neared the bottom he could see small fish swimming among the rocks. It was considerably darker near the bottom and he wasn't sure if he would be able to see far enough through the haze to spot the object of their search.

"Just how large is your craft?" Tim inquired.

"It's about three meters long, two meters wide and a meter high," came the instant reply.

"That's not very big for a space ship," Tim thought, as he swam about the bottom, mesmerized by the experience he was enjoying.

"It is only a compartment vessel used for evacuation in the event of an emergency," the alien conveyed. "My main craft is many times larger, with all the necessary equipment and supplies to sustain a flight of about five hundred earth years."

"Holy cow! Just how long do you guys live, anyway?" Tim asked, curiously.

"Some entities from my world will live ten of your centuries," came the matter-of-fact response.

Just then, a silver gray object shaped like a stepped on cigar appeared in front of Tim. It was sitting with its nose partially buried in the ocean's floor. It showed burn marks over most of the visible exterior and a crack was evident that ran diagonally front to rear and left to right. There seemed to be a kind of heaviness in the message that came to Tim as the alien transferred his thoughts.

"It is as I feared. It broke up on impact. I doubt there is anything of use. We'll leave it and perhaps some day return and take it to the surface for a better inspection. For now, we might as well return to your home. I believe your mother is expecting you to be home for lunch. What time does that occur?"

Tim looked at his watch, thankful for this gift from his dad and remembering how his dad had said jokingly that it was good to fifty fathoms. He was a half-hour late and a long way from the dinner table. He wasn't sure just what excuse he would use to explain his lateness but he doubted that this was any time for telling the truth. "I'm glad you understand the necessity of secrecy, Tim. Sometimes an absolute truth can be more damaging than an unadmitted one," Hunter silently conveyed. Tim smiled to himself as he recalled the lectures he had heard all his life about always telling the truth and just as quickly as the thought crossed his mind, he heard Hunter say, "There are few absolutes in life, Tim, on this planet or anywhere else in the universe. If my travels have taught me anything, it is that nature varies little when it comes to the forces that drive the sense of reasoning."

Once back at the surface, Tim looked around hoping that he wouldn't have to explain what he was doing, or for that matter, how he was doing it. Luck was with them and they found themselves alone in a wide part of the bay. As he climbed back into the boat he saw the glossy appearance of his skin return to normal and read the thoughts sent to his mind as they inquired how he felt about this experience.

"Hunter, anytime you want to go swimming, just let me know. This was the single greatest thing I've ever done. What's next?" he asked, with all the patience of a normal teenager.

"Hold the phone, young Tim," Hunter answered with his version of a laugh. "We've got more serious things to work on for now," then added as an afterthought, "Was that the correct use of your phone phrase?"

"You're learning," Tim muttered out loud and then laughed.

They docked the boat and put away the gas tanks and anchor, then Tim hopped on his bike for a faster-than-normal ride home. He burst into the kitchen apologizing even before his mother had a chance to scold him for his being over an hour late.

"It's no big deal, Tim," his mother assured, "I knew you would be in as soon as you got hungry. I'm just surprised you made it this long. You didn't eat out somewhere did you?"

"No, and I'm starved," he replied as he sat down and started shoveling in the food his mother put before him. His appetite was usually quite good, as is common for most teenage boys, but today he was doing justice to the several courses his mother offered him. As he was draining his second glass of milk his mother shook her head and said,

"It always amazes me how much you can put away and still stay so skinny, but it pleases me to see you have such a healthy appetite."

"I went for a short swim," Tim added as an explanation for the wet trunks he had dropped on the floor by the back door. "Swimming always makes me hungry, especially when the water is so cold."

"Isn't it just too cold yet to be in the water?" his mother asked with concern.

"That's why it was a short swim," Tim replied, hoping the story would sound plausible.

"Well, just to be on the safe side, I want you to take a dose of your allergy medicine," his mother advised. "If you'll remember, you got a bad summer cold last year after having gotten in the water when it was still too chilly." Reluctantly, Tim swallowed the syrupy sweet liquid and shook his head making a face in the process.

He knew that he and Hunter had to locate Torg and that time was of the essence so he asked his mother if it was OK for him to go back up to Mr. Whitney's, since he had missed seeing him this morning.

"Oh, I'm glad you reminded me. Mr. Whitney dropped by this morning to ask if your dad was going over to the mainland but I explained he had a conference to attend in Bangor with some Air Force people at the International airport. The old gentleman hasn't been feeling well and he thought your dad might fly him over to Bangor so he could get a checkup. I offered to take him to Eastport but he said he might drop by Doctor Sloan's on the north end. He hasn't much faith in old Doc Sloan but he is getting a little worried. I think it may be his heart, the way he talked. He said, for the past two days he gets so weak and light-headed. If your dad flies back to Bangor tomorrow maybe he can take Mr. Whitney with him."

Tim thought he and Hunter had best get up to Mr. Whitney's before the old man came in contact with Tim's dad, so he asked his mother if it was OK for him to run up and check on their old neighbor. Given her consent, he walked outside, jumped on his bike and headed up the island road toward the little white cottage.

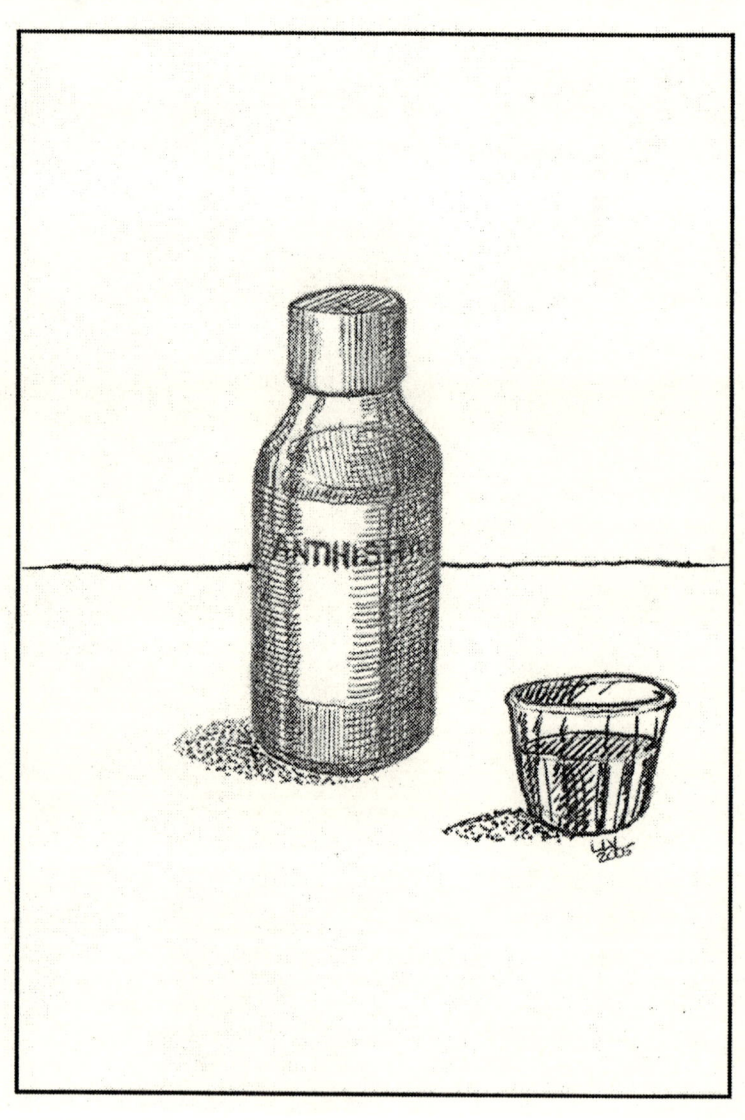

Chapter 4
The Secret Weapon

"Do you think Torg is the source of Mr. Whitney's illness?" Tim asked Hunter. There was no reply. Tim stopped pedaling, and coasted slowly to a stop. He hesitated a moment and then said out loud, "Hunter, are you there?" A low humming sound, almost like a groan sounded in Tim's head.

"What happened just now, Tim?" came the weak, halting reply.

"I don't know what you mean," Tim said. "I just asked if you thought Mr. Whitney's illness was caused by Torg?" Hunter slowly replied,

"I don't recall the question, Tim. The last thing I remember was your mother giving you something that tasted very sweet. And then I was aware of your speaking to me audibly."

"Do you mean you fell asleep?" Tim inquired, almost laughing.

"No. We do not sleep as humans do. Something rendered me unconscious, and I have only experienced that condition one other time when my host was shot by a neutron laser," Hunter went on to explain.

"Well, I think it's safe to assume I wasn't shot with a laser gun so something else had to zap you. Do you remember mom giving me the antihistamine?" Tim asked.

"I recall your experiencing a sweet taste and then, nothing until you spoke," came the reply.

"Well Hunter, old man, all I can say is, you can't handle your antihistamine," Tim answered with amusement. Several seconds of silence followed as both considered the implications of what had just happened. Then Hunter said, "Tim, you're thinking the same thing I'm thinking. This might be a way to immobilize Torg."

Tim considered the idea, then replied, "This telepathy thing is a little confusing, Hunter. You said we were thinking alike yet I'm not entirely sure which thoughts are mine and which are yours. I feel like I'm talking to myself in my head sometimes, and I'm hearing an echo."

"Well, Tim," the alien answered, "if it helps, just consider whether or not you knew the answer or idea that had just come to you. If you did not previously know the information, you can assume it was from me. If you already had this information in your memory banks then I'm either agreeing with you or you're talking to yourself. If it's the latter, then it's all right, as long as you don't make a habit of it, since that would surely confuse me. Is that sufficiently clear?"

Somehow Tim got the impression Hunter was doing the alien version of a grin and thought there may have been a touch of space humor in his companion's reply. As Tim headed on up the road towards Mr. Whitney's, the two Siamese sleuths began to hatch a plan of attack, but first they had to find the hiding place of their prey and immobilize it.

Tim knew that there was a drug store on the north end of the island and they agreed it would be best to go to Mr. Whitney's armed with a bottle of antihistamine-laced ammunition. He parked his bike on the sidewalk and made his way to the cold medicine section of the pharmacy. As he picked up each bottle, he and Hunter analyzed the contents on the labels until they came to one that contained the highest dosage of their secret weapon. He handed it to the owner along with a five-dollar bill. The pharmacist rang up the sale and handed it back to Tim in a sack bearing the drug store's name. As Tim turned to leave, the man behind the counter said with a word of caution,

"Don't be riding your bike right after taking that, if it's for you, because it can make you sleepy and your reflexes will be slower than usual. There's a warning right on the bottle, so heed what it says."

"Yes sir," Tim replied, "I've seen what this stuff can do. I'll be careful." Tim was grinning as he left the store, knowing that at last they had a plan of attack. He pointed his bike down the road and toward the moment of confrontation he and Hunter had been seeking.

As soon as he saw Mr. Whitney sitting on his porch with the big golden dog at his feet, he felt both relief and a sense of alarm. It reminded him of a showdown. Two enemies were going to come face to face. Who would draw first and who would shoot the straightest?

"Tim," Hunter asked, "what do you mean, *draw first* and *shoot the straightest?*"

Then, Tim realized he was letting his youthful imagination of cowboys and gunfights become direct communication to his new semi-subconscious. "Forget what I just said, or rather, what I was just thinking," Tim replied aloud. "You're going to have to get used to the fact that not every thought I think is a word I would speak, if I was speaking to someone who could hear."

"But Tim, I can hear every word you say, just as I can hear your thoughts," Hunter replied with a bit of confusion. Tim gave that some deliberation, then replied with added thought,

"Well, I guess you'll have to figure out a way to divide the thoughts I have between those directed to you and those not directed toward anyone. Those will be just random thoughts for my own benefit. Does that explain it?"

"I'll work on it," came his silent answer.

As Tim walked up on the porch, the old man greeted him with an invitation to sit and have a glass of tea. Tim could see that the old man was having a glass for himself and saw this as the perfect chance to slip him some of the secret weapon. Tim accepted the offer and the old man got up and walked inside to pour a glass for his young guest. Hunter immediately outlined his plan. He instructed Tim to find an excuse to touch the old man after the old gentleman had consumed some of the doctored drink and it had a chance to be absorbed into his system. Hunter wanted the effects to be felt by Mr. Whitney and Torg, if the alien was present. This would provide his entrance into the temporary host. Hunter said once he had determined if Torg was indeed in Tim's neighbor, he would appear on the forehead of the old man, as a sign that he was ready to return to Tim's body. With their plan formulated, Tim dumped an ounce of the medication into the old man's glass, which was sitting on the table between their chairs. He had just put the bottle back into his pocket when Mr. Whitney returned with Tim's refreshment.

"Mom says you're not feeling so well," Tim said, with a note of concern.

"She's got that right, my young friend," answered the old man. "It might just be a flu thing because I was feeling just fine until two days ago. I started getting so tired and feeling like I could hardly put one foot in front of the other that evening after we talked on the beach."

Tim had an idea that might speed things up a bit. He reached into his pocket and brought out the bottle of medicine and said, "Mom thought the same thing, you know, about it being the flu, so she sent you a bottle of the stuff she pours down me and Dad whenever we start coming down with something. It always seems to work for us," and he handed the bottle to his old friend.

"Well, that was mighty thoughtful of her, Tim. You tell her I said thanks. I'll go take a spoonful right now." With that the old man got up and went inside his house.

"Good thinking, Tim," Hunter said. "With what he has in his tea plus what he is taking now, Torg should be unconscious for quite a spell, if he is using Mr. Whitney as a host."

The old gentleman came back out of the house and sat beside Tim on the porch. Tim was being careful not to touch him until the time was right. The two sat talking for a while giving the double dose time to do its job. Finally, Hunter told his host to shake the old man's hand as a gesture to leaving but then stand a moment to talk some more. Tim did as instructed and Hunter transferred to the old man with the handshake. The boy continued standing on the steps telling the old man that he had taken a boat ride yesterday out in the bay. He knew that the older man had been an avid fisherman at one time and thought this would be a subject that could hold him there until Hunter was finished. It seemed to Tim that Hunter was taking an awful long time to get the information he needed and it was getting difficult for the boy to think of things to say. He doubted that there was any kind of confrontation going on inside the old man since the old gentleman was showing no signs of distress. Quite to the contrary, he seemed very alert and had a clear tone to his voice that Tim had not heard before. Suddenly, the old man stopped in the middle of his sentence and grew quiet. Tim could feel the hair standing up on the back of his neck and he became especially tense. Then the old man took a deep breath and said with a big smile,

"You know something, Tim, I think that medicine you gave me is going to do the trick. I'm not the least bit tired. As a matter of fact, I feel just great all of a sudden. That is some powerful stuff. Even my sinuses are clear and it's been a long time since I could say that."

A shiny spot appeared on the old man's forehead and Tim took the cue to shake hands once again and say good-bye. He held onto his neighbor's hand until Hunter told him he was ready to leave. As he was getting on his bike he happened to look around and noticed that the big Labrador dog was nowhere around.

"Mr. Whitney," Tim asked, "where's Blondie?" The old man looked around just then noticing that the dog was gone.

"Beats me, Tim," he said, "she was here a while ago. Must have run down the beach aways. She'll be back. She never stays gone long." Tim wanted to get away now as he had a lot of questions for Hunter.

"I'll watch for her," he called over his shoulder as he pedaled down the road. As soon as he had gone a short distance from the little white cottage, he began asking questions of his unseen guest. "What happened? Was Torg using Mr. Whitney? Were you able to kill Torg, or do you do that? How come Mr. Whitney suddenly got so full of energy? Did you do something to him like you did to my knee?"

Hunter didn't reply right away and when he did begin answering Tim's questions, it seemed as though the alien was tired, for the replies came slow and deliberate.

"There was considerable damage done to the old man's circulatory system. Some was probably just due to his age but a lot of it was the result of Torg consuming much of the old man's life giving elements. I repaired his blood vessels by cleaning out all the built up matter in them that didn't belong there and removed the excess calcium deposited in his joints. I managed to screen through his organs and clean out all the deposits in them that would be harmful to his over all health. During that process I was being grateful that my species doesn't have a skeleton. I'm sure the old man will feel a lot less old from now on."

"That's all great," Tim interjected with excitement, "but what about Torg?" Tim froze as he registered Hunter's reply.

"Torg wasn't there."

Chapter 5
Strategy for Attack

A lot of different scenarios were playing through Tim's mind as he and Hunter considered their next move. While Tim took them back home, he looked all around for the big blonde dog as he pedaled toward their house but the animal was no where in sight. They both thought that Torg had most likely reentered the dog's body in an attempt to find a more mobile host, one that could take him off the island. This was a fairly large population to screen given their limited access to the people who came here for their summer vacations. There could be as many as five or six hundred at the peak period of activity, which was now. Their biggest help was that they were on a more remote part of the island with only about a dozen or so in residence. If Torg was able somehow to make the dog venture a mile or so to the north end then it was a whole new problem. Tim asked Hunter if the alien could influence the dog to make the long venture away from its usual home.

"Torg might cause the dog to feel hungry resulting in its traveling in search of something to eat, but not knowing the dog's habits, everything is pure speculation."

Tim parked his bike in the garage and walked into the house. His mother was sitting in the living room reading and Tim inquired about his dad's whereabouts.

"Has dad gotten back from his trip to Bangor, yet?" Tim inquired.

"As a matter of fact, he did. He got in about an hour ago, but Mr. Whitney's dog was lying in the garage when he pulled in. We thought perhaps, the old man had dropped by for a visit but when he didn't show up, your dad took the dog back up to his place."

Tim's heart sank with the realization that his dad had likely became Torg's next host. He could hardly think straight as he mumbled an excuse to go to his room. Once there, he shut the door and sat down heavily on his bed.

"What do we do now?" he said softly but audibly. The boy's concerns were obvious to Hunter as he monitored his vital signs.

"First of all, you must stay calm, Tim." Hunter warned. "We have several elements in our favor. First, we know where Torg most likely is. He doesn't know where I am. And he doesn't know I have an assistant." Tim perked up at that thought. He mentally imagined a shingle hanging over his bedroom door that read,

'Tim Northfield, Assistant Space Ranger and Detective'. It had a nice ring to it. Hunter interrupted this imaginative scene.

"Tim, what was that all about? The Space Ranger thing?"

Tim replied with a smile,

"Do you recall my telling you that some of my thoughts would not be a direct communication to you, but rather, would be for my own use? Sort of, private, like? Well, this is one of those times."

Hunter paused a bit, then replied, "OK, but can you give me some kind of a warning when you are going to do that, so I'll know not to pay any attention?"

Tim considered the question and then tried to explain the process of human daydreams.

"It just doesn't work that way, Captain. It would defeat the purpose of spontaneous thinking if we had to stop and analyze it all first. You're just going to have to go with the flow on this one. You'll get the hang of it. I'm sure you're a quick study."

"I'll try," came the reply with a sense of struggling resolve.

Hunter outlined their plan of attack.

"We know that Torg was not in the old man when you gave him the medication, so he will not be forewarned as to its effects. That makes it still, our best weapon. We think he will be using your dad as a host. We have to get him separated from your dad as soon as possible before he can harm him. Now, do you have any gasoline like we encountered at the boat?"

"Yeah, Dad keeps a can in the garage for the lawn mower," Tim replied. "You're not thinking about pouring gas on my dad are you?"

"No! Not on your dad! On Torg," Hunter went on to explain. "Given its properties for being so very acidic as well as highly combustible, I believe it will be one of the few things that can put an end to the centuries of killings and agony that Torg has inflicted on different species across the universe. If we can cause a state of unconsciousness in Torg, I might be able to enter your dad's body and remove him. Once outside your dad, it will be up to you to use the gasoline. Tim, it means you will be ending a life. Is this something you think you can do?"

Tim thought about it for a moment, then said with confidence, "Yeah, I don't see a problem. Fortunately, you guys look like a bowl of Jello. Now, if you happened to look just like a little baby, or say, a pretty girl, well then, we might have a problem." Hunter paused before making a reply to his host's answer and then silently uttered,

"I'll try to handle the logic of your answer, Tim, but your concept of my species does give me some concern. I would hope that you would not view me with the same lack of regard simply because I am also of a life form far removed from your own."

With a note of apology in his thoughts, Tim assured his guest that no such problem existed with the explanation,

"Oh no, don't worry about how I think of you, Hunter. I saw how Torg treated Mr. Whitney and his dog. He is the typical concept of a parasite. He lives off his host without any benefits to that host. Torg has shown that he cares nothing for the welfare of the one who sustains him. On the other hand, you have healed me, aided me, even made it possible for me to swim like a fish, which incidentally, I want to do again soon. You repaired the damage to Mr. Whitney caused by Torg and then improved his health beyond anything our doctors could have ever done. No, you've proven yourself, Hunter. Trust me. I do not see you in the same light I see Torg."

There was a sense of relief in the reply that Tim registered from his alien passenger.

"I'm glad you feel as you do, Tim. It is vitally necessary that a condition of trust must exist between us if we are to be successful in what we hope to achieve. Now, let's go wait for your dad to return."

They went into the kitchen and Tim poured himself a glass of milk from the refrigerator. He sat down at the table next to a platter full of fresh baked cookies and proceeded to do what all young boys do under the circumstances and given the opportunity. The detective and his assistant went over the steps they would have to follow to affect their plan. At one point, Tim got up from the table and went into the garage to locate the can of gas his dad kept for their mowers. He found it to be about half full, making it contain nearly three gallons of fluid. He looked around, at Hunter's suggestion, and located a snow shovel, which he felt would serve their purpose.

"This should work just fine," thought Tim. Then he found the fire extinguisher and set it where he could get to it quickly. With all his props in place, Tim returned to the plate of cookies and a second glass of milk and waited for his dad to get home. He hoped that Torg was not as prepared as he was. Suddenly a thought occurred to him.

"Hunter," he began thinking anxiously, "How are you going to keep the medication from affecting you when you go in to get Torg?"

"That's a good question, Tim," came an immediate reply. "I've been working on that and I think I know the solution. What does the medication do to you when you take it," he questioned.

"I get sleepy," Tim replied.

"Exactly!" Hunter came back. "Now think. What will counter-effect this sense of lethargy?"

"A stimulant of some kind, I suppose," Tim returned.

"OK, Tim," Hunter went on to explain. "I've been analyzing the effects on you caused by the foods you eat. With the exception of the very sweet medication that completely left me unconscious, I find that when something is sweet to your taste, it tends to speed up your metabolism and also makes me more aware of everything. The ingredients your mother uses to produce the sweet taste seems to be what speeds things up."

"Well, that's no big secret," Tim casually said. "It's the sugar. Sugar gives you a burst of energy. Here, let me show you." He took a spoon, dipped up some raw sugar out of the bowl on the table and dumped it into his mouth. As it began to melt Hunter conveyed that this would be their defense against the antihistamine. He wasn't sure how long the affect would last but he only needed several seconds, at most, to complete the extraction. There was one problem, though. The sugar would likely revive Torg from his unconscious state, just as it protected Hunter. But, it was a problem they would deal with when the time arose.

Now, with most of the details worked out, the pair waited for the sound of the family car to pull into the driveway. Their sense of uneasiness increased as the minutes passed and the father had not returned. Finally, Tim got up and went into the living room where his mother was making repairs to a pair of Tim's pants.

"Mom," he asked, "did Dad say how long he was going to be gone?"

"No," she replied. "He just said he was going to take Blondie back to Mr. Whitney. But, I look for him home anytime now."

"Would it be OK if I took my bike and rode up to Mr. Whitney's to see if Dad's still there?" Tim inquired.

"Just don't stay out too late," she responded, "and if your dad is still there, tell him supper will be ready in about an hour. I hope you didn't ruin your appetite by eating all those cookies, young man."

"Mom, that was just an appetizer," Tim replied, as he shot out the door. With the help of his new internal assistant, Tim made it to the white cottage in record time. He breathed a sigh of relief when he saw his dad's car parked next to the cottage, and he hopped off his bike and took the front steps two at a time. He was just about to knock when Mr. Whitney opened the door and invited him inside.

"Come on in and join the party, young fella," the old man said, as he offered Tim a glass of iced tea. Tim's dad was sitting at the small dining table in the one room that served as a kitchen, dining and general visiting area.

"Henry tells me that your mother sent over some cold medicine that made a new man out of him. It sounds to me like some kind of miracle snake oil, or something," Tim's father said with a smile.

Tim sort of stammered as he explained, "It was just some of that red, sweet stuff she keeps around when my allergies are acting up. It's an antihistamine, I think she said."

"Well, it's done wonders for me, I mean to tell you," the old man added with excitement. "I ain't felt this good in, well, I don't remember just when I did feel this good. Even my arthritis doesn't hurt. I even did a little jogging down the beach today. Now, it's been ages since I could do that. I'm gonna' keep a bottle of that stuff on hand all the time."

"That usually makes me sleep like a baby," Tim's father replied. "I never knew of it giving someone a kick."

"Well, I'm not staring a gift horse in the mouth. I'll just keep some on hand and hope it continues to do the trick," was the older gentleman's response. Tim interrupted the conversation long enough to deliver his mom's message concerning supper and his dad rose to leave.

"Thanks, Will, for returning my dog," the old man said as Tim's dad headed for the door.

"It was my pleasure to help, Henry," came the reply, and then he added, "By the way, is Blondie beginning to have accidents with her bladder since she's getting a little age on her?"

The old man thought about the question for a moment, then replied, "Not that I've noticed, Will. Although I thought she had peed on me yesterday but when I looked closer I was mistaken. Why? Did she do the same thing to you?"

"Well, sort of, I guess," Tim's father explained. "I thought she had wet on my front seat when I was bringing her back but when I stopped here at your place and looked more closely, it didn't look wet anymore. I wasn't sure just what had happened so I thought I'd ask. I don't think any harm was done," he added as an afterthought. "Well, we better get to supper or Marie will be on my case. Tim, do you want to throw your bike in the back of the truck and ride with me," he asked, as they headed out the door.

"If it's OK with you, Dad, I'll just ride my bike home. It's not that far." The boy tried to disguise the feeling of concern that was overtaking him and he didn't want to get too close to his father since he was sure that Torg had now found his newest host.

As Tim pedaled his bike toward home, he and Hunter began to hatch a plan to rid the universe once and for all of this alien who had been the subject of an intergalactic hunt that had been going on since shortly after Christopher Columbus landed in the new world. It was beyond Tim's comprehension what kind of dedication it would take to engage in so intense an endeavor that would consume five centuries and cover a distance to what we might consider the edge of space. Tim listened intently as Hunter explained what his existence had been like following Torg from one star system to another, and realizing that every time Torg slipped away again, it would mean that another trail of dead bodies would be the mute testimony to the rogue alien's passage. He had to be stopped and it looked like earth was to be the place. Without conveying the thought to Tim, Hunter just hoped there would not be a trail of dead earthlings in Torg's wake, especially since it might be within his young host's family. He was bound by tradition to keep his host from harm, but he was beginning to feel that he had little control over the emotional injury that would result from Tim losing one, or worse yet, both of his parents.

He felt he was running out of time and options.

The prospect of never being able to leave earth again was also an ever-present dilemma he didn't like to consider. But it was becoming more real with each passing day.

Chapter 6
Making Plans for a Midnight Attack

By the time Tim walked into the family kitchen, his mother had their supper on the table and his dad was sitting in his usual place reading the paper. At one point he put the paper down and rubbed his eyes, making the comment that he must be more tired than he thought.

"I'm having trouble focusing to read," he said, to no one in particular. "Maybe I need to see if it's time to get a pair of those little reading glasses that just set on the end of your nose. They do give a sort of intellectual look, don't you think?" he chuckled. The humor of it was lost on Tim as he recognized the symptoms.

"Did you see any writing or anything, Dad?" Tim inquired.

"No, Tim. Things just got blurry. What do you mean, did I see any writing?"

Tim realized the danger of the question even as Hunter was cautioning him to be careful what he said, as Torg was aware of all that was going on around the kitchen table that evening. "I meant, could you clearly see the words in the paper?" he corrected.

"They just got blurry for a minute. It was like I had a film over my eyes. I rubbed them and it went away. It must have been like you the other night when you came out of your room and asked us to look at your eyes. You said you were having trouble, too. Remember?"

Tim was beginning to feel uncomfortable with this line of questioning so he excused the situation by commenting that it was just one of his usual allergies and it cleared up with some of the medication he usually took. This reminded Tim's dad of the comments of Mr. Whitney who had taken some of the same medicine at his wife's suggestion, as explained by Tim. He turned to his wife, who was setting the meal on the table, and said, "Oh yeah, Henry Whitney said that cold medicine really did the trick. As a matter of fact he said it gave him a new lease on life, as he described it. And he was going to keep a bottle around all the time. That was his exact words."

Tim was feeling flushed with this conversation and he wasn't sure how he would explain his telling the old man the medicine had been sent by his mother, when she was totally unaware of any of the happenings of the last couple days. He was greatly relieved to hear her say, "Well, that's nice. I'm glad he's feeling better. Now let's eat while it's still hot."

Tim breathed a sigh of relief when he realized he wouldn't be called upon to explain his actions. He imagined that Hunter was doing his variation of the same thing.

As they sat eating their meal, Tim was struck with an idea for a good attack on their unwanted guest.

"Dad," he said, "maybe a dose of that same medicine would do you some good. It cleared up my allergies and certainly helped Mr. Whitney." Tim's father didn't respond right away. He seemed lost in his own thoughts, then abruptly looked over at Tim and apologizing, asked his son to repeat what he had said. Tim frowned at this somewhat unusual behavior and Hunter silently cautioned Tim once again to choose carefully his words, as he was convinced that Torg's presence was having an influence on the father. Speaking with careful deliberation, Tim repeated his earlier idea. "Well, I thought how well that allergy medicine had helped me and Mr. Whitney, so maybe it would also help you."

Hunter then offered a suggestion that Tim relayed to his father.

"Why don't you take some just before bedtime, then, it won't interfere with your evening?"

Tim and his unseen guest knew that the timing for taking the antihistamine was of the utmost importance. If taken too soon, the affects might be worn off the other alien before Hunter would have a chance to achieve an extraction from the unsuspecting host. The timing was crucial but it had to be handled much like disarming a live bomb.

One wrong move could mean someone could be hurt or perhaps killed. Hunter had explained to Tim earlier that if it came down to a matter of strength and cunning in a combat with Torg, then the advantage was on the side of Hunter's adversary. Due to the training and principles that had been a part of Hunter's life for the past several centuries, he doubted that he would be able to actually kill Torg, even though this concept might not be accredited to the rogue alien.

The job he had originally set out to do was to capture Torg and return him to their home planet for a trial by their high tribunal. If that tribunal decided that rehabilitation was not possible, then he would be placed in a sealed chamber where he would have to remain until the end of his natural life. Given the life span of their species, that could be a long, long time. But they were not on Hunter's home planet and it didn't look like that would ever come to pass, so a trial was a luxury they could not afford to provide Torg. It created an unprecedented dilemma for Hunter. He couldn't simply ignore the timeless traditions that made up his psyche. They were as much a part of him as was the electron gelatin that flowed through his life system. He had explained these problems to Tim during a moment of silent communication and Tim made reference to an earth saying about, 'When in Rome, do as the Romans do'. This translated for Hunter to mean that here on Earth he might have to do something totally unnatural for him as well as for his entire species. He wondered if he would be up to it when the time came, and if things continued on course, that time was growing very near.

After their meal, Tim's father went into his office to work on a report, which he intended to present to the aeronautical board in Bangor the next day. Tim walked into his father's office on the excuse that he was curious what he might be working on. The sudden interest in his work was both surprising and pleasing to the father and he immediately went into a lengthy and detailed explanation. Tim's real purpose in the intrusion was to find an excuse to get his dad to take a couple of doses of the 'alien tranquilizer', so his concentration on the report was less than keen. However, the essence of the father's report was of great interest to Hunter as he too, listened to the account outlining a program for inter-space communication between Ground Control and the astronauts in an orbiting space station.

Hunter now began to realize the scope of Will Northfield's work. This was both good fortune as well as bad. It had the potential for helping Hunter make contact back to his home planet and contact a ship to come get him. But, it also gave Torg the same possibility. And Torg was the alien control for this host. The showdown was approaching and the outcome was far from certain. Hunter realized that if he failed now it would likely cost the lives of these humans who had provided him the host body his species required. To fail in this responsibility would be a failure to fulfill the very purpose for which he and his kind were dedicated. This was not merely a contest to see that the right and just might prevail. It was a struggle to preserve the purpose of life for this alien species. In the next few hours, much would depend on how well Hunter had learned his task.

Tim sat listening to his father explain the workings of the communication system his company's engineers had created. Most of what his father said was Greek to Tim but Hunter understood it all quite well, even though he thought it a bit simple or at least simple by his species' standards. For Tim it was like listening to two records playing at the same time, as he heard not only what his father was saying, but also what comments Hunter was making. Surprisingly enough, he heard both conversations separate and distinct. He decided to ask Hunter how that was possible but then remembered that Hunter had already received his question since it was done as a thought. He wasn't sure if he would ever get used to that.

After Tim's father finished his lengthy explanation, he asked Tim if he got the general idea what it was all about. Tim asked him how it differed from the message that originates in the standard home computer and is sent through cyberspace. His father was surprised at the comprehension of his young teenager, so he went on to explain how the telephone lines provided the channel for the messages while it took a directed laser beam to carry the voice of Ground Control to the men in the space station. At Hunter's insistence, Tim acted satisfied with the answer and rose to excuse himself from his father's office.

As he reached the doorway, he turned and added, matter-of-factly, that he would put the bottle of allergy medicine on the stand next to his father's bed. He hoped his voice sounded casual as he reminded his father how well it had worked for himself and for their neighbor. His father thanked him for his concern and gave him an assurance that he would give it a try. Tim felt a little lighter as he headed for his own room, knowing that their plan was now under way.

Hunter was well aware of Tim's concerns, having a few of his own that he chose not to share with his young host. Entering and leaving a host was a simple matter for his species in that they merely absorbed through the pores of the host's skin, but he had never tried to make this transition while, literally, pulling another alien along. He wasn't sure if it could be done without alerting the host that something very strange was happening to him. He wanted Will Northfield to remain asleep since he couldn't predict what his reaction might be if he encountered the aliens coming through his skin. He doubted it would be a pleasant experience for any of them, including Tim, who would be trying to explain his part in it all. No, it had to be done without arousing anyone, most especially, Torg.

Tim sat at his desk staring at his computer without actually trying to view the rapidly changing features on the screen. He was allowing Hunter to scan through the myriad information on the Internet while the alien controlled Tim's fingers. Just as Hunter had made Tim an Olympic style runner, he now had his fingers flying over the keyboard so fast they were a blur. Hunter had explained that in addition to being a space cop it was also his duty to collect whatever information might come his way about the other species and cultures that he might encounter in his travels. This was an opportunity so fortuitous that Hunter could hardly believe his luck. He not only had a host that accepted his presence but even welcomed it. The real bonus was having landed in a family that was involved in the sort of work that could get him back to his home planet. He was amassing all the information he could about this culture's history, current affairs, and technology. But the area of greatest interest, aside from going back home, was learning of the customs and personal interactions of this species. It was obvious the information logs of Earth kept on his own planet, and which were a part of every student's education there, was seriously lacking.

Hunter had come to believe that all of Earth's inhabitants were wholly war-like and lacked the psychological makeup for any kind of peaceful existence. By observing Tim and his family and reading the texts that ran across the screen on Tim's computer, Hunter was beginning to get another picture of these creatures in their early evolutionary state. Now, he was most anxious to return to his home planet with this newly acquired information. But first, there was this thing with Torg.

Hate, like all emotions, was unknown to his species. Situations and beings were just accepted as they were and dealt with accordingly, but this thing with Torg was creating an electrical activity in Hunter's control chambers and it was beginning to resemble an obsession closely akin to what Hunter discerned as hate. He wondered if his kinship with the Earthling was affecting his perception. He made a note of this for a future report, ever optimistic that he would someday be able to deliver it.

Chapter 7
Final Confrontation

It was midnight when Tim walked quietly down the hall to his parents' bedroom. Once outside their door, he stopped and listened for the sounds that they would assure they were deeply asleep. Tip-toeing to their bedside, he picked up the bottle of antihistamine and checked the line he had made on the side indicating the amount before his father's taking it. He smiled when he realized his father had taken to heart the improvements in Mr. Whitney. He had taken at least two ounces, or a double dose. He put his hand on the bed and watched with amazement as the glistening, shapeless organism, known as Hunter, exited his hand and absorbed into his father. As agreed in their plans, Tim went out to the garage and picked up the snow shovel and a large heavy-duty plastic bag and carried them back in the house and took up a position just outside his parent's bedroom. Hunter's instructions were for Tim to remain in the hall unless his parents awoke and alarm was indicated, which they both felt would be the case should either parent catch sight of the two aliens.

The minutes dragged by and Tim was tempted to open the door, partly out of anticipation and partly from curiosity. Then he saw it. At first it looked like water might be running from the other side of the door onto the carpet in the hall. Then it took on a glossy appearance and began to grow in size, both in width and it height, until it was a mass of rolling, pulsing gelatin. It moved surprisingly fast and had a marbled appearance. Then it began to separate. Half of it had a light blue cast and the other half was more green. With one quick motion, Tim took the snow shovel and scooped up the green one and dumped it into the plastic bag and followed it with a similar motion dumping the blue one in on top of the other. Then he picked up the bag and quickly but quietly took it out to the garage. Tim decided that he should not confront the two aliens inside the garage for fear of waking his parents, so he carried the bag of squirming gelatin out to his basketball court, which enjoyed a slight illumination from the streetlight in front of their house. He went back in the garage and got the can of gasoline and the CO_2 fire extinguisher that he had previously set aside.

He could feel his heart pounding in his chest as he considered his next move. Although he had rehearsed it several times in his head, this was different. This was the real thing and he had no prior experience for what he was about to do. Come to think of it, no one on the face of the Earth had ever had this experience before. And when it was all over, he knew that he could never tell anyone, not that they would believe him if he did.

His hands were trembling as he untied the plastic bag and laid it on the ground and stepped back. He picked up the fire extinguisher and pointed it at the bag which was moving slightly, as first one mass, then the next, emerged. Tim stood there transfixed by the sight of these two shapeless masses as they moved around on the concrete, coming up to each other, and then backing away. Suddenly the green mass turned and moved toward Tim. It occurred to him that this could be Hunter who wanted to resume his position within Tim to combat his foe, Torg. He hadn't expected that there would be a difference in their colors and Hunter had failed to explain this one crucial element. Not knowing which was which, and realizing that a mistake in identifying would likely be fatal, Tim backed away from both aliens.

Without a warning, the blue mass combined with the green and began moving toward the can of gasoline. Long tentacles of green gelatin shot out behind the greater mass and imbedded themselves in the concrete halting the movement toward the can. Tim began to understand the drama playing out before him.

He picked up the fire extinguisher and gave a short blast to the two combatants. When the blast of cold CO_2 hit them, they separated and each coiled up into a tight ball about the size of a large grapefruit. Tim immediately scooped up the blue mass and dumped it back into the plastic bag and threw it out into the yard. He then grabbed the gas can and poured it over the green alien. There was an audible sound emitted from the alien as it slowly melted into a thick hard substance resembling melted plastic. He turned and picked up the plastic bag inserting his hand inside. The light blue gelatin disappeared into his hand and Tim's face broke out into a broad smile as Hunter conveyed the message,

"A job well done, Tim," which was the sign Hunter said he would give when it was all over. Earlier in their planning, when Tim showed concern and doubts, Hunter had assured his host that he would be the first to congratulate his young companion when success was at hand. And five hundred years of pursuit had finally come to an end with the help of a fourteen year old Earthling. Hunter knew his companions back home would never believe this story, but he was still most anxious to give them all the details.

Conclusion

With the evidence of the adventure cleaned from the basketball court and the remains of Torg burned to ashes in the bar-b-que pit, Tim returned to the house and went quietly to his room.

"Well, Hunter," he sighed, as he flopped down on his bed, "do you think anyone would believe that we just saved the universe?" And he laughed out loud.

Hunter was slow in replying, as he tried to weigh his words and not diminish Tim's efforts, yet keep things in perspective. Finally he conveyed the thought, "What you did tonight showed bravery and great intuition. You discerned which of us was which, and you removed a very destructive force from the universe. But Tim, regardless of what you or I did, the universe would have continued on with or without us. However, you definitely made it a safer universe. And by the way, how did you know which was which? Was it when I tried to keep him from reaching onto you or when I tried to drag him into the can of gas? I really would have killed us both before I would have allowed him to escape or invade you. But, just what was your clue?" Tim grinned as he thought his answer.

"Neither one. It was his color. Anyone who ever went to a science fiction movie here on Earth, can tell you that little **green** men from outer space are always the bad guys."

Printed in the United States
49929LVS00005B/502-552